SESAME STREET
CTW
A GROWING-UP BOOK™

BIG BIRD CAN SHARE

By Dina Anastasio/Illustrated by Tom Leigh

A GOLDEN BOOK • NEW YORK

Published by Golden Books Publishing Company, Inc., in cooperation
with Children's Television Workshop

One day Big Bird woke up very early. He rubbed his eyes, stretched, and looked out of his nest. There, on his mailbox, were a brand-new pail and shovel.

Big Bird looked at the tag tied on the handle. It said, "Dear Big Bird, I think you'll know what to do with this! Love, Granny Bird."

"Gee, I wonder what Granny Bird means," he thought.

Big Bird walked down Sesame Street, hugging his new
pail and shovel to his feathers.

"Hey, Turkey!" called Oscar the Grouch from his can. "What are you going to do with that pail and shovel?"

"Oh, hi, Oscar," said Big Bird. "Well, I, uh…"

"Slimey and I could use them to dig for worms," Oscar said. "How about it? Heh, heh."

But Big Bird didn't want to share his new pail and shovel with Oscar and Slimey. "Gee, Oscar, not now. Sorry." And Big Bird walked away fast.

Big Bird almost bumped into Ernie and Bert.

"Hello, Big Bird," said Bert. "Look at all the bottle caps we've found for my collection."

"Those sure are nice bottle caps," said Big Bird.

"And that sure is a nice pail and shovel," said Ernie. "Could we borrow your pail to carry the rest of the bottle caps?"

Big Bird hesitated. He didn't want to share his new
pail and shovel with Ernie and Bert.

"Never mind," said Bert. "I'll bet you're going to make
a sand castle in the sandbox. We'll come to see it later."

Big Bird walked through the park to the playground sandbox.

"How do you make a sand castle?" he wondered.

Big Bird sat down in the sandbox. He scooped sand into his pail with the shovel, and then poured out the sand into three piles.

"I wonder if this is what Granny Bird meant," he thought.

"Hello, Big Bird," said Grover. "I could not help but notice that you are trying to build a cute and wonderful sand castle." Grover sat down in the sandbox. "If you put water on it, the sand will stick together. Let me take your adorable little pail and fill it with water from the fountain."

"Well..." said Big Bird.

Betty Lou stepped into the sandbox. "Would you like to share my watering can, Big Bird?" she asked. "You can use it to sprinkle the sand with water. Then we can use your pail to make towers."

"Oh, thanks, Betty Lou," said Big Bird. "I guess you can share my pail." He took her watering can and handed her his pail.

Big Bird sprinkled the sand with water, and Betty Lou showed him how to use his pail to make sand shapes. She packed wet sand into the pail and turned it upside down. Then she carefully lifted the pail off the sand.

"Oh, Betty Lou," said Big Bird. "That's great!"

"Oh, I am so excited!" cried Grover. "Building in the sand is fun!"

"Hey, everybody!" Big Bird called to his friends. "Come and look at the neat sand castle we're making with my new pail and shovel."

Cookie Monster and Prairie Dawn came over to help.

"This castle needs more delicious towers!" cried
Cookie Monster.

"This fort needs windows and doors," said Prairie
Dawn.

"Let us make a tunnel between our castles," Grover
said to Big Bird.

Other friends came to help build the sand city.

"This castle needs a moat!" said Betty Lou, and she began to dig.

"And a bridge to go over it!" said Herry Monster.

Ernie and Bert came over to see what everyone was doing.

"Look at the neat sand city, Ernie!" said Bert.
"Right, Bert," said Ernie. "But I think it needs some special decorations, don't you?"

"Good idea, Ernie," he answered. "How about some
shiny Figgy Fizz bottle caps on the turrets?"

When all the castles and forts and bridges and roads were finished, everyone stood back and admired the magnificent sand city.

"Gee, everybody!" cried Big Bird. "Our sand city is so beautiful!"

"Honk, honk, honk!" honked the honkers.

"Thank you for sharing your pail and shovel with us, Big Bird," said Herry Monster and the others.

Big Bird smiled. "This is what Granny Bird meant!"